Haunted
Hawaiian Nights

Haunted
Hawaiian Nights

Lopaka Kapanui

Mutual Publishing

ISBN 1-56647-758-1

Cover art by Roy Chang
Design by Jane Gillespie

First Printing, September 2005
1 2 3 4 5 6 7 8 9

Mutual Publishing, LLC
1215 Center Street, Suite 210
Honolulu, Hawaii 96816
Ph: (808) 732-1709
Fax: (808) 734-4094
e-mail: mutual@mutualpublishing.com
www.mutualpublishing.com

Printed in Australia

For Glen

Table of Contents

Foreword

If storytelling is a dying art, Lopaka Kapanui has the power to wake the dead. As a poet and spoken-word performer, stage and film actor, professional wrestler, Hawaiian immersion schoolteacher, kumu hula in training, and ghost tour guide, Lopaka tells stories in a myriad of venues and genre. Stories follow him like a string of nightmarchers trudging relentlessly along their predetermined path. Sometimes he tells them to share the burden of horrifying mysteries that live inside his head. Sometimes he tells them as an invitation to others to drink from the well of our collective subconscious. Always, he tells them as a means of communion with his fellow human beings; storytelling, next to breaking bread, is the oldest, most primal, most generous form of sharing.

In this book—his first published collection of stories—Lopaka explores territory familiar, but always fascinating, to him: ghost stories and tales of the supernatural. As the guide for his late mentor Glen Grant's ghost bus tour, Kapanui has spent countless (often sleepless) nights at the Chinese graveyard in Mānoa and the infamous Morgan's Corner in Nuʻuanu scaring the wits out of his customers.

Along the way, he has collected new stories. Some have been given to him as gifts from people who have hidden their dark secrets for years until finding the right person to trust and confide in. Others were found discarded along the roadside, in need of dusting and polishing, but gems nonetheless. Most are recollections of personal experiences, memories he himself had been wanting to share, but only when the right place and time came along. This book is that place and that time.

So if you have been thirsting for the beauty that lays beneath the surface, for the mysteries of that "other" world which exists on the flip side of our mundane, day-to-day existence, turn the page and drink. The well is on the other side.

—Robert Pennybacker

Preface

The more believable ghost stories come from people whose daily lives are mundane. Often, they live on the edge of poverty, and an evening meal in each others' company is a luxury. Their lives are not defined for them by soothsayers or psychics; indeed, their lives are for the most part unseen and unrecognized. Ghosts are the least of their concerns.

So when these people tell me ghost stories, I am always interested, if not entirely convinced. If you ask me how I know when someone is telling me the truth, I would answer simply: I look for the change in his face, the tears in his eyes, the pitch of his voice. I keep a sharp eye out for goose bumps. Chicken skin. These are dead giveaways, and these are some of their stories.

Acknowledgments

To Marguerite, my wife, I appreciate all that you do. And to our daughter Hiwalani, may our traditions live through you. To all of those ancestors who have inspired this work, without your permission and the permission of your descendants, these stories would not have been possible. Thanks must also go to Robert Abuel for his compassion and guidance, and to his family for their love and aloha. To my late mother Angie for her love. To the brothers of Koʻolau Lodge for their support in all my doings.

The Chiefs of Julius Ahern

Julius Ahern Elementary School is on the leeward side of the island, on an old depot road. It's been nearly swallowed now by a suburban city called Waikele. But once upon a time, it was a lonely place, and Waikele itself was arid and flat and often desolate. And it had legends.

One of those legends involved two chiefs who were brothers. The older brother was the chief of Oʻahu, and he lived in Waikele. His younger brother lived in Waikīkī.

The younger brother hated and envied the older one. He wished to rebel and take over his brother's throne, but he took his time, and this is how his plan unfolded.

Back then, chiefs often amused themselves by catching tiger sharks, using men as bait. By law, the sharks were caught under the direction of the kahuna.

One day, the younger chief caught a shark of impressive size. He then divided the shark from head to tail, removing the innards and saving the skin. Its teeth were left intact, and a frame built to match the body of the shark. When all this was completed, a place was carved in the shark's belly where the young chief could sit. And there, silently, he sat alone, kept company only by his plot to overthrow his brother.

▼   ▼   ▼

The older brother lived quietly in Waikele, but his kahuna was struck by a dark premonition. "Ahuhea ʻoe e ka lani!" he said to the chief. "It has been revealed to me in a vision that your younger brother has come into possession of a fish."

The older chief looked steadily at the kahuna. "You look too troubled," he said, "for one who is concerned only with a fish."

"He has thoughts," said the kahuna, waving his arms wildly. "He will come to see you, bringing the large fish with him. He will ask you to take the fish, leaving it in your care. His messenger will arrive soon. When he tells you of the request, refuse him."

"Why," asked the chief, "should I refuse to grant my brother his wish?"

"Because," said the kahuna sadly, "he will kill you. For it is a human fish he brings. He wishes to rebel against you and seize your kingdom."

The chief shook his head in disbelief, and could only wonder why the kahuna was so adamant.

"Aye," said the kahuna. "You will suffer a cruel death. But I myself have a narrow path to keep." And he left quickly.

Not two weeks had gone by when an envoy arrived from Waikīkī with the message, just as the kahuna had foretold. After hearing him out, the older chief agreed.

The messenger raced back to Waikīkī and told the young chief what his brother had said. At once, the young chief ordered stones to be bundled into ti leaves, securely tied to look like gifts for the older chief. A mānele carrier was fashioned for the shark, to be carried on men's shoulders. Save for a very few in which the young chief had full confidence, no one was aware that he himself would be inside the shark.

All the people of Waikīkī, Honolulu, Kapālama, Kalihi, Moanalua, Hālawa, and Wahiawā went along, all carrying stones wrapped in ti leaves.

Meanwhile, the older chief sat waiting for his brother's arrival, eager to see the size of his catch. He had prepared food for all. As the sound of the procession grew nearer, the kahuna fled.

The young chief's commanders began to pair their men off, each with a bundle of poi. They walked arm-in-arm, preceded by the shark, and they shouted "E 'Ewa e, e kui na lima! E 'Ewa e, e kui na lima! 'Ewa, go arm in arm!"

Suddenly, effortlessly, the older chief's five houses were surrounded, fifty deep, and the line had not yet ended. Then everything stopped, and the young chief emerged from the shark, commanding his army to unwrap the bundles and throw the stones at his older brother's household. The chief and all his kingdom were killed in minutes, and some of their bodies saved for bait. The younger chief took over and ruled for years and years.

As time went on, this land would have the name Ke-one-kui-lima laula-'o-'Ewa" or "Going arm-in-arm on the breadth of 'Ewa." As time passed, a sugar mill would be built there. Around the mill there was a town, and a school as well.

Milk Deliveries

The Julius Ahern Elementary School, it was rumored, was built over a graveyard or heiau. There is no one left who can say for sure. Part of the graveyard had surely been uprooted for sugar cane and houses. At any rate, the school itself was named after the sugar mill's manager, Julius Ahern. His daughter went to that school and survived into a ripe old age, something Hawaiians call "puaaneane."

For the milk drivers of Silver Field Dairy Company, the school is haunted, and they would avoid it if they could. They've heard too much from the older drivers—about strange goings-on in the cafeteria, among other things—and they take unusual care to prepare new drivers.

The recommended precaution is not elaborate; it is in fact quite simple. Drivers take along a compact CD player with headphones. When they get to the school, they drive their trucks straight up to the rear door, put on the headphones, and turn up the player full blast. When they get out of the truck, they are not to turn off the engine and they must leave their headlights on. They are then told to load their hand trucks as heavily as possible, moving quickly to the freezer and back out again, and upon completing delivery, to leave immediately.

▼　▼　▼

Freddy Williams is a Vietnam vet, who has seen it all. A few years back, he signed on with Silver Field. He passes his probation and becomes familiar with all points on his delivery route, and has been given the Ahern precautions. One night, he has to cover for a sick driver at the last minute at Julius Ahern, and he forgets his player.

It's about four in the morning. The truck idles as its headlights illuminate the dark cafeteria. Both doors are wide open, and Freddy walks his last load into the freezer.

Suddenly, he hears the crashing sound of pots and pans dropping to the floor, then shattering dishes. He runs from the freezer, pausing long enough to notice that the cafeteria is pristine, unblemished, everything in its place.

He shakes, and hurries toward his truck, but as he passes the sink, he sees a can opener turning slowly by itself, prying open a can of peaches. Blind with panic, he runs faster, nearly forgetting to shut the cafeteria doors.

He feels the same kind of fear he had in Vietnam, the kind that gives stupor and superhuman strength in equal measure, and he tosses the hand truck with one hand into the cab. And then he realizes that the engine is off. He reaches down near the steering column to start it again, and finds the keys gone. They are not in his pockets. "Dammit!" he screams.

He unclips the flashlight from his belt and, on his hands and knees, shines the light under the truck. He hears a jingling sound above, and stands upright, very slowly. Above the driver's seat are his keys, floating in the air.

"Sching, sching, sching!"

They drop onto the seat. Sching!

Freddy runs and ends up in front of a supermarket on Farrington Highway. He uses a pay phone to call his supervisor.

"Hey, Freddy, why you no use your two-way radio?" the supervisor asks.

Freddy snaps. "Come get your truck," he says. "I quit!"

"Whatchoo mean you quit?"

Breathing deeply, Freddy tells the whole story.

There is silence on the other end. Finally the supervisor asks him calmly, "Did you wear your headphones with your CD player?"

"No. I forgot. Besides, you neva' tell me why I gotta wear those stupid headphones anyway."

"Freddy, before you step into the cafeteria at that school, you put your headphones on, you turn the volume up real high. You just deliver the milk. You no look right; you no look left. Just straight ahead. You won't hear anything—not the pots and pans, or the fireballs, the nightmarchers, the headless woman, and the ghost—and then you leave!"

Sanity insurance, of course. Freddy gets the week off with pay. He returns to work as though nothing had happened, and is relieved to find that his deliveries would be at a 7-Eleven just outside of Kailua. He arrives at 1 A.M, finishing up about five to two. It will be two o'clock when he reaches the traffic light at Kapaʻa Quarry Road, and he is alone on the road—no traffic either way, almost too quiet. As he waits at the light, he thinks briefly of the headphones, which he'd forgotten again, but no matter this time.

Suddenly he sees something moving out of the corner of his eye. In his rearview mirror he sees a moving reflection, which slowly comes into focus. She is an old, bent Hawaiian woman, with a shock of white hair and an equally old and faded white dress. Suddenly, he sees her on his running board.

He will remember later that his face and hers touched forever, only for a second. He will remember jumping to the passenger side and screaming and will never forget the odor—an ancient, musty smell —and the woman's withered fingers gripping the inside of the door like a cane spider, inching herself toward the seat.

The woman's eyes are wide and alert, but timeless and deep, and her mouth turns down awkwardly as she begins to speak. She has an enormous voice.

"You can give me one ride?"

And Freddy will remember screaming at the top of his lungs. He will never know when he stopped; he will recall his white knuckles on the steering wheel as his truck barrels into the darkness of Nu'uanu. He will always remember the cacophony in his cab, knowing later that it is coming from him.

Four hours later, Freddy is back at Silver Field, surrounded by his supervisors and two HPD officers. He'd called them, fearful now only that the old woman had fallen off the truck, onto the road, been hit, run over, please God, no...

In the end, the police reports yield no evidence. No witnesses. No sign of anything. Vaguely relieved, Freddy says to himself that he will never again drive without headphones.

▼ ▼ ▼

He has them on the seat two weeks later for a scheduled run to Julius Ahern. He drives to the building as usual, smiling at the short stout woman dressed in an old-fashioned nurse's uniform. She wears nylons and has on far too much lipstick.

He can hear Crosby, Stills, and Nash from the headphones to his right. The woman does not smile back at him, but instead seems to shake her head in disapproval. Thank God, he thinks to himself. This is his last Ahern run, his last load at the school before he moves up to driver supervisor.

"We're trying to find our way, back to the garden...." And Freddy sees another woman, tall, skinny, Hawaiian, wearing an official blue shirt. She has salt-and-pepper hair tied in a ponytail, and wears slippers, and is cupping her right hand to her mouth. Carefully, he removes the headphones he had unconciously put on, hearing "I am yours, you are mine, you are what you are."

Freddy looks at the woman. "Sorry," he says. "Where's the woman who was just here?"

"What woman?" Freddy describes her, but she still seems perplexed. Then she bites the bottom of her lip. "Wait right here. I'll be back in a minute."

It seems like more than a minute, but she returns with something under her arm, a photo album maybe. She walks toward Freddy, and holds a picture to his face. "This the woman you saw?"

"Yeah, that's her. School nurse? Cafeteria manager?"

"No!" She shakes her head vigorously. "This was the cafeteria manager. She's been dead five years now. I'm the cafeteria manager now. That's why I was trying to ask you a question."

"Ask me what?"

"I was asking who let you in the building. I'm the only one with the key. I was running late, and I was supposed to wait for you so I could open the door for you."

She is calmer now, and deliberate. "Now I understand. You see, Mrs. P.—this woman—was my boss. My God, she was soooo strict and she could be a real taskmaster. The one thing she never stood for was tardiness. Man, if you neva' had one good excuse for being late, you get the riot act. Huuuu! She used to make us cry. So das why she came open the door for you. She knew I was late."

Stunned, Freddy asks, "If you no mind the question, how she wen die?"

The woman took a deep breath. "She died right over dea," pointing to the door where Freddy had seen her earlier. "Heart attack. Waiting for one milk truck."

So the headphones don't work all the time. But Freddy advocates their use for all the drivers he trains now. He wonders if Ahern is still haunted, and if an ancient Hawaiian woman appears at night at Kapaʻa Quarry Road, and about cafeteria managers that look like nurses. Sometimes the drivers ask him, and he shrugs noncommittally and tells them they'll have to find out for themselves, and to always keep their headphones close by.

Norman

My friendship with Norman lasted ten years. It was one of those friendships that was somehow both casual and close. We might not see each other for six months or a year, but when we met, it seemed that it had only been a day or two.

This meant that we always had a lot of catching up to do. For my part, I was never able to find out exactly when or why he came to Hawai'i and how he made a life for himself. He would answer me vaguely and change the subject.

In April of '82, he called me one night to share some sake he'd gotten from a friend in Japan. I went to his Wilder Street studio. He prepared the hot sake in small teacups.

The wine relaxed Norman a bit—he was by nature guarded and evasive—and I had to assume that he listened to me with great interest as I told him about breaking up with my girl at McDonald's.

But he interrupted me out of the blue. "You know, I haven't talked about this in years. When you think about it, it's been a hell of a long time.

And for me, it comes back to me only in bits and pieces. Maybe because I'm afraid to remember the whole thing all at once. Who knows?"

I had suddenly stopped caring about my old girlfriend, and nodded at him to continue.

▼   ▼   ▼

"When I first moved here, I found a room to rent from this Hawaiian woman in Kalihi. She was originally from Molokaʻi, but she moved here as a young girl, got married, and had a daughter. The daughter moved to the Mainland and wound up marrying a local boy she met in college. But that has nothing to do with anything. Anyway, the woman's name was Mrs. Manuahi, and I loved her. She became my Hawaiian mother. The funny thing was this—after her husband passed away, she became a Buddhist, of all things. So every morning and every evening she would chant to her scroll in her altar. She tried to get me to chant with her, but it really wasn't my thing back then. I guess I was too much into myself. I was working full-time at GEM Store daytimes and taking some early morning classes at Dillingham Community College. And I'd just gotten into this theatre production of *Jesus Christ Superstar.* I didn't have a big role, but I could dance well enough to be one of the principals in the front line. That was cool.

"Anyway, the guy who played Judas in the show was a Hawaiian guy named Pohai. We had eyes for each other right away. But there was nothing we could do besides flirt. The director was a guy named Chapel, a heavy hitter in the theatre world here, and he had a strict no-fraternizing rule for the show.

"One evening, I got to rehearsal early, and the theatre was empty. I walked down the stairs to the dressing rooms when someone appeared out of nowhere and dragged me to the alcove, trying to tear my clothes off. I was scared, and I let loose with a punch, and when I did, I recognized Pohai. He let go of me right away and ran into the dressing room. I followed him, and saw that his left eye was swollen and badly bruised. He screamed at me to get out and leave him alone. I tried to explain, but it didn't do any good. I guess I realized then how fragile he was.

"Meanwhile, Chapel had heard something, and came down to the dressing room. Explanations don't come easy when you're dealing with a guy like Chapel, and Pohai just stood there with nothing to say. Finally, I piped up and told Chapel that we had been roughhousing, and things got out of hand. I knew he didn't believe me.

"When the rest of the cast arrived, Chapel did a funny thing. He called on all of us to form a circle on the main stage, all holding hands. He told everyone my version of the story, almost verbatim. Almost theatrically, Pohai took off his sunglasses and exhibited his shiner while everyone gasped.

"Now here's the part that's really strange. Chapel ordered Pohai to apologize to me in front of everyone. Man, Pohai was fuming! If looks could have killed, Chapel would have dropped dead then and there, and I probably wouldn't be here either.

"I guess the long and short of it is that Chapel knew exactly what had happened. He probably knew Pohai from way back. And even Pohai, who could be a prima donna, didn't dare cross him. Chapel's productions were the gold standard for Honolulu.

"Anyway, the rehearsals continued without incident. Pohai's eye healed. His ego did not. Then one night, Chapel called me into his office. When I entered, I was shocked to find Pohai already there, and I almost ran away. But Chapel shut the door and motioned for Pohai to speak. He was the soul of humility. He told me how sorry he was, and as a token of apology, he gave me a pair of dance shoes—the right size and style—and another wrapped gift he said I should hang in my bedroom when I got home. All was forgiven. Pohai lightly insisted that I put on the shoes right away, so I did.

"That night I pulled into my driveway, and Mrs. Manuahi was on the porch. She offered me some beef stew if I was still hungry. As I got out of the car, a sharp pain hit my lower back, so intense that I couldn't move. Good old Mrs. Manuahi was one strong woman, and she picked me up like a rag doll and carried me into the house. She took me upstairs and laid me flat on my stomach. Then she removed my new shoes and began massaging my back. That woman had some kind of magic, because within a minute or so, all the pain was gone. But I was exhausted, and I showered and went straight to bed.

"The next night was open—no rehearsal—and I went out with some friends to the old Royal Sunset Drive-In. Don't ask me why, but I decided to wear my dance shoes to the movie. Everything went fine at first. Then I had to use the bathroom, and on the way back, just as I was opening the car door, something grabbed my ankles and yanked my feet out from underneath me. I landed flat on my ass. This time, I really couldn't move, and my friends took me home. They were concerned, but Mrs. Manuahi looked at me and the bruise on my back and waved them off.

"She removed my shoes again and looked closely at them. She looked at me grimly and said that someone had spit into my shoes. The pain, which was subsiding, had me looking even more puzzled than I was, I guess. She said that an evil person could curse my shoes by spitting in them, and freeze my back, maybe, or trip up both my ankles. She'd heard a lot of stories. So I told her everything. She nodded kindly, and then asked to see the other gift, which I'd forgotten to open.

"I got it out of the bedroom and unwrapped it in front of her. We both drew in our breath sharply as we realized it was a drawing of a man and woman together. Sex was explicit—nothing artistic about it at all. But we examined it closely, and realized that the man was raping the woman. It became very clear to both of us. Pohai had tried to rape me.

"The first thing Mrs. Manuahi did was to take the dance shoes and place them in front of her altar. She told me that the scroll in the butsudan had so much positive energy that it would send the curse on the shoes right back to Pohai.

"Then we took the drawing outside and set a match to it. It burned slowly, and at one point the flame stopped suddenly and formed a circle around the man's face. The face looked directly at us. It was Pohai's face. Then the flame continued, twisting the face and the paper grotesquely and turning it all to ash.

"Chapel called me late the next afternoon, and his voice was very slow, deliberate, and matter-of-fact. He told me that Pohai had died the night before. He had been standing on his apartment railing watering his plants, some of which were hanging. He'd slipped off the railing, caught his shirt on the hook, enough to break the fall, but enough also to twist his shirt around until he suffocated. The neighbors said they heard a loud screaming at the time he died. 'Like the devil,' one had told the police. Another neighbor, who lived two floors up, said she'd heard a strange buzzing sound outside, and when she looked out, she saw what looked like a blue ball of fire streaking directly toward Pohai's place.

"There were no rehearsals that night, and the obituary appeared in the paper the next morning. Turned out that Pohai wasn't his real name at all. His real name was Pōpōahi, which I looked up. It means fireball."

Neither of us had touched the sake. We toasted each other silently, and I realized it was late. I took my leave. I knew I'd think about his strange tale until we'd meet again in a few months or a year.

He Malama Pū'olo

He malama pū'olo means a keeper of bundles, one who keeps objects—like human bones, pieces of wood, locks of hair, bits of excrement. The bundle-keepers are not benign. They send their bundles in a spirit of malice to gain control over someone, or to curse them.

The tradition is an old one. Ancient warriors would collect the bones of their enemies after battle and send them to rivals, bringing misfortune and doom to them.

These days, bundle-keepers are ordinary people. They seem normal, not clinically psychotic or even possessed by evil spirits. They are often quiet and unassuming, not calling attention to themselves—the sort of people who, in a crowd, are forgotten.

But a bundle-keeper could very well be your best friend or, even worse, a member of your own family. This way, he can get very close to you, and you are none the wiser until it is too late.

It's a little difficult now to obtain a person's bones or excrement, but hair is easy to come by. Failing that, a bundle-keeper sends something of his own disguised as a gift. It may be presented in person or in a roundabout way, through friends or the post office.

The only precaution you can take is this: If you know someone who absolutely does not like you at all, and he offers you a lei, do not accept it.

High School Graduation

Joleene Kalanihea, for reasons she never revealed, never cared for her mother's cousin Pūowaina. Pūowaina disdained her, she thought, and whenever they were thrown together, they behaved with icy courtesy toward each other.

Everyone in the family attended Joleene's high school graduation that year. It was a grand occasion, full of pomp, full of circumstance, and full of fun. And at the end of it all Joleene was buried under a sea of lei.

Usually, lei—even a sea of lei— sit lightly on the shoulder. But Joleene noticed two different colored kīkā lei, one purple, the other orange and black. She couldn't quite take her mind off of them.

She wore the orange and black lei to the party, drinking and dancing with joy. She barely noticed the odd sensation on the back of her neck, and would just readjust the lei every now and then.

She was scheduled for ear surgery the following morning to correct a blockage. The doctor had told her that she would only be in the hospital for a day, and home rest after that.

The surgery was a breeze, although when Joleene awoke she was still a bit dizzy from the anesthesia. Sitting up was harder than she thought, but she managed to get herself out of bed and make her way slowly to the bathroom. There was an empty chair at the end of the bed, draped over it was the same lei that she had worn last night.

It was the first time she had actually seen it; it was a plain cigar lei, like many others. And suddenly, the back of her neck began to itch again, like it had last night. Now and again, through the fog of the anesthetic, she thought she felt someone's fingernails scratching it lightly. It also felt like someone was pulling her hair.

On the way back to bed she ran her hand over the back of her neck, and she felt a knot in her hair that had not been there before. Slowly, mechanically, still medicated, she stood in front of the bathroom mirror trying to clear out the tangles. She then pulled the rest of her hair over the front of her right shoulder in order to see the knot, but it was just out of her sight. She remembered a hand-held mirror that her mother had packed for her, and she finally saw the knot. It resembled a perfect box, with the sort of patterns one would see in a lauhala mat. She was startled by a voice: "Who did that?"

She turned and saw her mother. "Ma! Try knocking next time!"

Her mother seemed oblivious, and began trying to unravel the knot with no success. "Try wash it out in the shower," she said, but Joleene remembered that the doctor had ordered her to keep her hair dry.

"Okay, then," said her mother. "Try a shower cap," and Joleene agreed so long as she kept the shower head at waist level. It was a good idea. Even after the bath and prep for surgery, she still smelled like cigarettes and old beer, and the hot water, soothing and steady, melted memories and troubles away. It occurred to her suddenly that she was now legally an adult. She heard her mother say,

"Eh, hurry up in there!"

Joleene stepped out of the shower to dry herself, put on a clean hospital gown, and made her way back to bed. As she settled in, the doctor walked into the room and looked at Joleene strangely. "What? What is it?" she asked.

The doctor was stern. "Why do you have that shower cap on?"

"Oh," said Joleene. "I just had to bathe, and you told me not to get my hair wet."

The doctor, a busy and irritable man, relaxed a bit. "Ah. Good idea. Now take it off so we can look at the results."

He examined her ear carefully with a light and suddenly seemed perplexed, then angry. "Joleene, what the hell have you done?"

"I took a shower with a cap on, just like I told you."

"You sure you had the cap on?" She nodded.

"Then look at your hair." Joleene placed her hand on her head. Her hair was soaking wet. She screamed loudly, and her mother, already suspicious of hospitals, began whispering something to the doctor. The doctor took another look at her ear, thought a bit, and said, "Okay. We'll keep her here a few more hours, check her again, then you can go home." He looked weary as he left.

She had her own bedroom, and her friends came to visit, often singly, in pairs, or in groups. They all noticed that she did not seem like her old self. She showed all of them the knot in her hair, and asked them questions. All were genuinely surprised. Joleene knew, finally, that none of them had had anything to do with it. She knew it in her gut. Each of her friends tried to undo the knot and none of them could budge it. Every now and then, she felt the tugging again, as though the knot was making itself tighter.

Her mother had called her brother Roddy, who knew about things like this, and Roddy promptly advised her to cut off the knot and burn it. After

Joleene's friends had left, she marched into her room with a pair of shears and promptly removed the knot with a smile of maternal authority on her face. As she went down the stairs, Roddy called back to ask if she had received anything out of the ordinary recently. Joleene said no.

Downstairs, her mother placed the hair into a frying pan. Upstairs, Joleene began to feel the fingernails brushing up her neck again. Downstairs, her mother doused the knot with kerosene and set it on fire to a match. It burned quickly. Upstairs, Joleene suddenly began to break into a high fever, and her mother rushed upstairs with an ice pack and aspirin. As the hair melted into the pan, she went into convulsions, and her mother, a strong woman, held her down with all her might.

As the pan cooled off, so did Joleene, and she was soon sitting up in bed wondering if she'd missed a few friends. She was up and around in a couple of days, though still housebound, and her mother suggested opening her graduation gifts, which were piled on a rocker in the living room. Over the back of the chair they saw the kīkā lei again.

"Mom, who gave me that kīkā lei?" asked Joleene.

"I think was—oh yeah, was Pūowaina. You know, my cousin." And they stared at each other, blankly at first and then both nodded. Uncle Roddy would explain it to them later, but they knew. The lei itself was the curse, as it had not been given with love. It was meant to do harm. And as the curse was woven into the lei, so it then wove itself into Joleene's hair.

Some years later, Joleene and Pūowaina met at a family reunion, and Pūowaina attempted an embrace. Joleene grabbed her arms and pushed her away. "I know it was you who sent the lei to me and why you did it," she said coldly. " I do not accept your curse. I give it back to you."

Pūowaina was stunned and, for a moment, motionless as Joleene spun on her heels and walked away, free of the curse and the burden. Had she walked past Pūowaina and looked back, she would have noticed large patches of hair missing from the back of her head. When Joleene went home that night to her boyfriend, she hung an open pair of scissors over the front door of the apartment. She never told him why, and he had sense enough not to ask.

Unbroken Traditions

It seems unusual to some that a graveyard in the middle of downtown Honolulu takes up nearly a whole city block. Others find comfort in the fact that it is itself a part of Kawaiahaʻo Church.

To walk through it is to discover deep sadness and no little insight. Many of the headstones are of children, remembered with faded photographs. And many of them did not live to see their tenth birthdays. Churchgoers customarily place gifts on their graves at Christmastime.

One night, shortly before Christmas, a new security guard approached the graveyard from the back end of the church, near the playground. His name was Melvin, and he was a hardened veteran, whose twenty years in the military had made civilian life a bitter shock. He came across three women placing presents and a lei on the grave of a 9-year-old, named Peter Gregory Nahola. His headstone was a small one, in front of a tall acacia tree adjoining the playground, and a black and white snapshot of him had been placed just below his name.

The new guard was a surly man in the best of times. As the women greeted him and wished him Merry Christmas, he turned on them, swearing,

"Get the hell out of this graveyard. Take your presents with you!"

The shocked women tried to explain, but their words fell on deaf ears. The guard, to make his point, kicked one of Peter's presents off the grave toward them. One of them, enraged but frightened, said, "I'm gonna call your supervisor!"

The guard laughed, with bile in his voice. "Go den. Before you call him, I call da cops!"

The women disappeared, and the guard watched them leave, snickering. Nobody would mess with his graveyard. He turned back toward the playground and again toward Punchbowl. He felt a tug on his pants leg. He turned to see a small Hawaiian boy looking at him, bewildered.

"Why?" asked the boy. "Why?"

"Why what?" mocked the guard.

Another voice behind him, from another direction, said, "Why?" The guard looked around again; it was the same boy. He began to back away.

"Why did you do that?"

There was a hitch in the guard's voice. "Do what?"

And again he heard a voice, high-pitched, insistent. "Why did you do that?"

The guard, frightened, ran along the Punchbowl side of the cemetery. His eyes caught a photograph on a headstone—a picture of the same boy.

In addition to being surly, the guard had seen combat and was a martial arts instructor. He had not known real fear for a long time, until now. So he ran. He sprinted across the graveyard toward the corner of Queen and Punchbowl, seeking the safety of the street lights. But the closer he got to the lights, the louder the boy's voice became:

"WHY DID YOU DO THAT? COME BACK HERE!"

Disoriented and nearly deafened, he tripped hard on a headstone, then fell on another, and another. His knees, shins, and ankles were shredded, and he could feel the blood in his shoes. He had to keep running, and each time he started, the boy's voice, louder each time, would yell,

"WHY?"

The guard fell, nearly unconscious, to the ground, breathing rapidly, his heart racing. He looked up at the sky, and saw the rows of headstones. Finally, he said something he had never said in his adult life:

"I'm sorry! Whatever I did, I'm sorry!"

He waited for the worst, even though he was in the middle of a paved lane, three feet from freedom. He heard footsteps—adult footsteps—and sat up weakly. A policeman walked toward him.

The cop sat with him in the ambulance as they bandaged him and checked his vital signs. Apparently, some senior citizens in a home across the graveyard had called the police. They had all been awakened by the sound of screaming children.

The guard, bandaged, defeated, and contrite for the first time in his life, told the cop what had happened. The cop looked at him hard, and then shook his head over and over again in disgust.

"You stupid bastard. Who the hell you think you are? Man, you don't mess with these church women, and you don't push your weight around in a Hawaiian graveyard. I hate to say it, brah, but you got bus' up and you had it coming."

The guard nodded meekly, rubbing the bandages on his legs.

The next day, the three women arrived at the graveyard early, before the guard came on duty, with more gifts. And when they arrived, they had another, more present shock. On each child's grave was a new present, wrapped in haste but carefully placed, a note attached to each one. All the notes said the same thing: "In honor of the unbroken tradition." The notes were unsigned.

On Peter's headstone there was a lei of ti leaf and maile. His note was different, and said, "So you may never need to ask why again. Your friend, Melvin."

Ronnie Hightower

Her full name was Ronnette Hightower, but everybody called her Ronnie. Back in '91 we were both involved in a local theatre production, *Ola Waiʻanae,* and in it, we compared life in Waiʻanae in ancient times to life today.

After the show, we lost touch with each other. One day, out of the blue—it was March of '92, I think—everyone in the cast got an invitation from her for a weekend party. She lived at the Mākaha Plantation and had a large third-floor condo with a stunning view and enough room for thirty people.

By three in the morning at the party that weekend, most everyone was asleep. Ronnie motioned me over to a huge koa table in the middle of the room. I remember thinking that if Kamehameha himself had had a round table for his warriors, it might look like this.

"You know," she told me, "my kitchen is the most special place in the house." She paused, a bit pensively. "It's filled with magic," she whispered fiercely.

She'd been drinking tequila, and her eyes were wild and misty.

"Magic? How so?" I asked.

She looked at me intently. "The nightmarchers. They come through my kitchen. They start from Kāneʻaki heiau, way in back of the valley, and then they come through the golf course, all the way to Mauna Lahilahi. And they come right through this wall, right beside where we are now. They even walk through my refrigerator."

I smiled to myself and thought of *Ghostbusters*—the scene where a demon appears in a freezer. I knew Ronnie was drunk, but she was also matter-of-fact, and lucid enough to sense my skepticism. She went on.

"When I moved here a few years back, I was asleep one night and I smelled something rotten enough to wake me up. Man, it was bad! Then, when I came out of the bedroom, I heard drums. Not some guy in the upstairs apartment practicing, mind you, but a whole army of drums, so loud it damn near busted my ears. First I thought somebody must be playing that heavy metal crap on their stereo, but I knew right away it wasn't that. Especially when I turned around and saw lines and lines of Hawaiian warriors marching through my kitchen. They were five in a line, walking right through the wall as though it wasn't there.

"Next thing I knew, I felt a huge hand grab the back of my head, pushing me to the floor and holding me down. The more I struggled, the more useless it got, and all I could hear was the endless footsteps, the drumming—and that God-awful smell.

"Then it let go, just like that. Everything was normal again. From the look of things, nothing had happened. I asked my landlord, who's a haole guy, and he told me straight that it was the nightmarchers. A haole guy, mind you! I was surprised, but found out later he had the same problem in his place too."

She wasn't slurring her words, and her eyes burned with intensity. I began to wonder if she was drunk at all.

She went on, her voice clear as a bell. "It was like that for a while, always on the night of Kāne—the moonless night. Then one year my father made this table for me. Nice, yeah? I put it here because it was the only place it would fit.

"And since then, when they come on the night of Kāne, they march right through the table."

I whistled through my breath. "How long has this been?"

"Four years." She paused, stretched, and looked at me again. "Let me ask you a personal question. Okay?"

"Okay," I said.

"You ever been in a relationship where you were unfaithful?"

I'll never forget what happened next. I'm pretty close-mouthed and reserved, but I answered her freely, without hesitation. I had been—indiscreet on occasion. There was nothing I could do to stop myself, and I had to shake myself violently to keep myself from going into graphic detail.

"Oh, shit! I can't believe I said that!"

Ronnie was laughing, and I was getting irritated. "Ever since the nightmarchers came through this table," she said, "no one who sits here can tell a lie."

"For real?" I said, feeling embarrassed and a bit annoyed with myself—and her.

She nodded and smiled. "For real. That's how I found out my sister was fooling around with my husband. We sat here one night for dinner and it just came out, flowing like water. Man, the look on their faces! The same look you had on yours."

It was a terrible thought, especially since she was so beautiful. I began to wonder if Ronnie was maybe just a bit cruel. I wondered how many other confessions she'd collected at this table.

Eventually, though, I cooled off. Maybe there should be a place like that in every house, where people with nothing to hide had nothing to fear, and those who did would stay away—a modern kapu, portable, its sphere of influence limited. Besides, I wanted to hear more about the nightmarchers. Who was it, I asked, who'd held her head down to the floor that night? With that she folded her hands and began to cry.

"Hightower is my married name. My maiden name is Kalaniopu'u. While I was being held, over the sound of the drums I heard a name whispered in my ear—that of Kalaniopu'u. He saved me—he let me go."

The table had helped us strike a bargain, an even trade, a truth for a truth. As the Mākaha night turned into morning, Ronnie would tell me more about her life, including the precise spot in Pōka'ī bay in which her shark 'aumakua could be found. But that's another story, for another time.

Pele's Thirst
(Ko Pele Make Wai)

Whenever Mother needed a rest, we all went to Auntie Mary Greene's house in Kalaoa, in upcountry Kailua-Kona. We went there for the last time in 1991, and something happened there. She told me this story before she died in November of '92.

Mother stayed inside during our visits; the rest of us would be out shopping, or sightseeing, and every once in a while we would venture to Halemau'ma'u to pay respects to Pele, our ancestor and our deity.

Auntie Mary's house was soothing and cool, and winds would gently push back the curtains. Mother was resting in the back bedroom. She heard a voice, dimly at first, then louder. It was the sweet voice of a young woman at the front door. It had been many years since she had heard someone call out in such a way. "Huuui! 'O wai ka po 'e ma kēia hale nei?" Mother understood. The girl was asking, "Who are the people of this house?"

Mother got out of bed and went to the front door. On the porch, through the screen, she saw what she would later describe as the most beautiful Hawaiian girl she had seen in her life, peerless and without equal.

The girl's hair was long and full, jet black with 'ehu (red) streaks. Her skin was dark and flawless, and her face so naturally beautiful that any makeup would have detracted from it. She showed no fatigue, even though the Kona sun was unbearably hot. And she was barefoot.

Mother stepped outside and they exchanged warm alohas.

"Please," said the girl in Hawaiian. "I am thirsty. "Ice water? Please?"

Mother smiled and nodded. She went quickly to the kitchen and found the tallest glass in the cupboard, and went to the refrigerator for ice cubes. But the water in the trays was not yet frozen. Mother went to the front door and explained.

"Don't worry," said the girl, still speaking in Hawaiian. "Plain water will do." Mother went back to the kitchen, filled the glass, returned to the door, and handed it to her.

Mother told us that when the girl took the glass in her hand, a cold icy film formed over it. She drank without stopping, and gave the glass back to Mother. It was still cold and stuck to her fingers.

"Mahalo piha," the girl smiled. With that, she turned around toward the front steps and walked toward the end of the road. Beyond there was nothing but wild kiawe trees and ʻāʻā lava, unforgiving for bare feet.

Mother called after her to ask if she needed a ride. "No," said the girl. "My home is not far away. I will be there shortly."

"But where do you live?" asked Mother. The girl pointed in the direction of Hualalaʻi and the volcano. Mother gestured toward the car in the driveway, turning away for only a moment. When she turned around, the girl was gone.

The odd thing was this: it did not occur to Mother to tell the story until much later that night, after dinner. Auntie Mary listened intently. After Mother had finished, Auntie looked at her for a long time. Almost impassively, she said, "That was Pele."

Maybe it was. As it happened, everyone had decided to visit Halemaʻumaʻu that day. Perhaps Pele had noticed that one of her children wasn't there, and, concerned, had decided to pay her a visit.

"You see," Auntie Mary said to Mother, "it had nothing to do with the ice in the water. It was about the warmth in your heart." And Pele was satisfied, and disappeared into the volcano that she herself had created.

Papa is Home

We have a little apartment off Date Street, and I can tell you quite honestly that it's not haunted. That doesn't mean that we don't have visitors now and then.

Back in 2000, I was telling ghost stories at a Tae Kwon Do camp at Kalaeloa Beach Park. I had a captive audience of two hundred, complete with campfire; most were children. As the storytelling drew to a close, I decided to ask all of them to sit with me in the forest to hear the very last one.

To make the story come alive, I'd arranged with one of the dads to put on a monster mask I'd given him, and to jump out at the right moment. He was perfect. Never before and never again will two hundred people scream so loud and run so fast! Everyone had a good time, even the organizers.

When I got home that night, my wife was waiting up for me. She told me a strange story. While I was out, she was in the living room with a book, and she heard our daughter calling "Mommy?" from the bedroom. She went in to check on her and my daughter said, "Tell Papa to stop rubbing my back. I can't sleep."

"Papa's not home, baby," my wife said. "He's out telling ghost stories."

▼ ▼ ▼

At first she was frightened, but she soon concluded that whoever had been rubbing our daughter's back meant no harm. I went into the room myself and kissed my daughter good night. It was then that I smelled the pua kenikeni flowers. Then I understood. When my father was alive, he planted a tree in his yard and it bloomed all year round. Tūtū—my mother—loved them.

The first year after our daughter was born, the three of us slept in the living room on a futon. The air conditioner was out, so we slept in the area between the front door and the lānai. That way we always had a cool breeze coming through our apartment.

One night, while we were all asleep, I felt someone's foot under my back, nudging me hard. I woke up and saw my mother, visibly upset.

"Move you! Move the baby from this spot!"

In a daze I woke my wife and told her that we had to move the futon toward the center of the living room. She was too groggy to argue. With our daughter asleep on the futon, we moved it to the right spot and went straight back to sleep. Then I bolted up again, eyes wide open, waking my wife again.

"My mother was the one who told me to move the futon. She nudged me with her foot."

It was clear to me now. We'd been sleeping between the front and back doors of our apartment, something local families don't do, because the dead walk through there. It's their path. It was '96, and Tūtū had passed away in '93. I explained all this to my wife.

She looked at me a long time, then turned away and said "Good! Tell her I said fo' slap yo' head too!"

I didn't sleep well that night. I kept waking up to look around the living room to make sure Tūtū wouldn't honor my wife's request.

Going Home

Jenna Paʻapaʻana has had a lifetime of otherworldly experiences. She has plenty of stories, enough to fill a novel. She works as a masseuse.

Back in the 1980s, she told me, she worked at a restaurant on the old Kumulaʻe pond in Mōʻiliʻili. A banyan tree was one of the place's main attractions, and it was not uncommon to see local celebrities during brunch or dinner.

She worked as a cashier, in the back of the restaurant. At closing time, the only people left were Jenna and Russell, the manager. One night while she was closing out and counting money, she heard Russell in his upstairs office typing wildly on the old Underwood. She furrowed her brow as she closed the register, for she knew that Russell was a one-finger typist.

"So what, Russell, you taking typing class on the side?"

"No," said Russell, directly behind her. Jenna screamed and pointed upstairs. "Not...you?" she asked, shaking.

"You hear it too? I thought I was going crazy!" Russell's face was drained, his face as white as his eyes.

"Who's up there?" Jenna whispered.

"I dunno," said Russell. "I locked the door an hour ago."

Jenna tells this story with a smile and a shrug. She remembers that the restaurant had to hire a new security guard nearly every week, all because of a woman's ghost rowing a small boat over the pond.

▼ ▼ ▼

She neither shrugs nor smiles when she tells this story, though. One night she attended a lecture at the Bishop Museum. Nainoa Thompson was the speaker, so the hall was packed beyond capacity. But Jenna and her sister had arrived early and found seats.

Nainoa spoke with his customary eloquence about symbolism, about wayfinders, and the journey of the Hawaiian people toward self-determination. His speech was seamless and intense, and Jenna was annoyed by the sound of wailing and crying somewhere in the room. No one else seemed to notice it, but it was driving her to distraction. She couldn't figure out where the dirge was coming from; it seemed to be nowhere and everywhere all at once. She looked around. Her sister poked her in the ribs. "What are you doing?"

"You hear that?" asked Jenna.

"Hear what?"

And Jenna knew instinctively that she was the only one who could hear it. Soon it became so loud that she felt lightheaded, her stomach turning. She tried to concentrate. In her mind she asked, "Who are you?"

The voice replied—a young voice—in Hawaiian.

Jenna, in her mind, said, "I'm sorry. I don't speak Hawaiian. You have to talk to me in English or I can't help you."

The voice replied, in pidgin English, "I like go home."

"Where is your home?" asked Jenna silently. She was beginning to feel better.

"Captain Cook," said the voice. Jenna was stunned; her family was from Captain Cook.

"The Big Island?"

"Yes," moaned the voice. "I like go home."

Jenna was feeling disoriented again. "Who are you?"

"I'm one fish in one rock. Please take me home!"

Jenna was now dizzy, unable to concentrate. "Don't talk to me anymore. My head hurts!"

The voice obediently and sadly faded as it begged again to be taken home.

After the lecture, Jenna's head cleared a bit, and she realized that she must have been talking to one of the exhibits in the museum. But she had no idea which one. On the way home to Pauoa, she told her sister everything that had happened.

Her sister reminded her of her gift, of her affinity for the supernatural, something handed down from one generation to another among women. After what had happened, Jenna saw it as more of a curse than a gift.

And life for the Pa'apa'ana family went on as usual, until Jenna's sister went to Kona on vacation. She joined a tour of ancient sites. Then she visited the Mo'okini heiau to meet the kahu, a woman named Pearl Choi.

She told Pearl everything about Jenna's experience at the Bishop Museum. Pearl listened intently, scrawled something down on a piece of paper and gave it to her. "This is my phone number," she said. "Tell your sister to call me right away."

It was not until the end of the year before Jenna called Pearl. She learned that Pearl was on O'ahu at the Bishop Museum. She drove there, found

Pearl, introduced herself, and followed her to the breezeway and a small rock garden.

Pearl looked at Jenna intently. "Talk to the stone now. Let it know you are here."

Jenna relaxed, concentrated, and attempted to talk to the stone. But it did not speak to her. She gave up with a sigh. "It won't talk to me. Maybe you..."

Pearl waved her away. "I already have a stone that I talk to. And only I can talk to it, because it is my stone. This one is yours, and it will only talk to you. Try again. Clear your mind completely and it will talk to you."

Jenna tried again, breathing deeply. Then she heard a voice, faint at first, then louder. "I stay heah. Heah." She followed the voice for half an hour, and finally found it. It was a porous, charcoal gray rock shaped exactly like a fish.

Pearl told Jenna that she could tell the rock was not happy by its color. "When the rock is happy," she said, "it turns 'alaea—red. Now it must go back home to Captain Cook."

Jenna picked up the stone gingerly and started to hand it to Pearl, but Pearl would not take it. "Don't you understand?" she said, gently but a bit impatiently. "It's your stone. You have to take it home, not me!"

While Jenna cradled the stone gently, Pearl spoke to the curator for a long time. Much to Jenna's surprise, the curator agreed that whatever was best for the stone was best for everyone.

"Now," said Pearl, "when you take the stone, you must wrap it in a ti leaf. It has to be kept moist."

▼   ▼   ▼

The next morning, Jenna boarded a flight to Kona, with the stone in a small cooler. She had asked her sister to come along, just for luck. They landed in Kona, rented a car, and drove the stone home. When Jenna removed the stone from the cooler and unwrapped the ti leaf, she almost dropped it. The stone was red.

She held the stone up to her sister, who was still in the car, and her sister smiled. She walked out to the point where the memorial stood, stepped carefully over the wall, and returned the kupua stone to its home in the ocean.

She began turning around to go back and stopped dead in her tracks. From the top of the hill to a few feet in front of her stood ancient people of the land, looking. And it made sense now. Indeed, the stone was hers, and these people were her ancestors.

▼   ▼   ▼

As I mentioned, Jenna is a masseuse, and a gifted one. She has a level of skill and insight that allows her to see into peoples' bodies, diagnosing illnesses, recommending cures.

After she told me the story of the stone, she shared a few more small stories, then I had to get back to class. Usually, when we say goodbye, we hug each other. She was hesitant to do so this time.

Above the Reef

Manford Helumua's life was hard and his heart was heavy. He drove a school bus for a guy named Gouveia, a hard man to like, for over thirty-five years. Most nights after work, he could be found at Papa Walter's karaoke bar.

He told me once that he had no time for ghosts. Not that he didn't believe in them. He just didn't have the time to pay them any notice.

But as we sat outside Papa Walter's eating boiled peanuts, out of the blue he told me this story.

He grew up in Mākaha with his father, and everything they ate was either homegrown or caught. There was no playtime. As soon as Manford did his homework, he'd hop in the back of his father's pickup and head for Mākua. Then he and his father would swim out just beyond the reef off Nanaue. Manford would tread water, holding onto a bag, while his father went diving for their supper.

One evening, when Manford was nine, he held the bag, waiting for his father to dive again. They had a good catch already. His father dove down once more, and emerged screaming, "Swim! Swim! No look back!" His father's fear, which he had never seen before, stoked his own as they both swam for shore. They were not too far from the reef and were back on dry land in no time. Then his father tore the bag out of Manford's hands, fish and all, and flung it over his shoulder where it landed on the sand.

Grabbing Manford's hand, his father raced for the pickup and they headed home.

Manford, of course, was bewildered. When they got back to the main road, his father told him that when he dove the last time he saw a good-sized ulua right in front of him. He tried to spear it, but the fish was too fast. The spear missed the ulua and hit what looked like a huge reef bed. But when the spear hit, the reef curled to the left and swam away. It was a shark. It was the biggest shark his father had ever seen, and so old that its back was full of barnacles. He wasn't about to wait to see if the shark was going to return.

Manford's father would never know that his son had seen the shark many times, often when they were swimming back to the reef. It always seemed to swim below them, maybe a few feet down, just following. It felt as though they were being watched over and cared for.

As he grew older, Manford knew that this must have been their 'aumakua. After all, fish were always plentiful when they dove. And the other sharks never bothered them.

▼   ▼   ▼

There were young girls at Papa Walter's, some of whom worked on a cruise ship. They had a low tolerance for alcohol, but Manford was a kindly man. I remember that night they dragged him back into the karaoke bar to sing an old Hawaiian standard in a high falsetto—something only he can do. It's called "Blue Darling" or something like that.

I remember also that my watch read 2:30 A.M., and wondered if my 'aumakua was going to protect me from my wife's fury.

Ronnie Hightower II

In late '92, Ronnie invited me to camp at Pōka'ī Bay. We got there about four in the afternoon, and began simply enough. We ate, drank, and sang. The barbecued chicken was about the best I'd ever tasted. Her boyfriend had come along, and he owned a canoe.

"Let's go out," she said, motioning toward the canoe. "We'll just go out past the breakers and come right back." She usually got what she wanted, and her boyfriend shrugged and smiled at me.

He steered the canoe while we paddled in a wide arc, preparing to make our way back into the bay. Then suddenly Ronnie yelled, "Hoe! Paddle!" I put my head down, leaning forward as far as I could and dug the paddle into the water and straightening up, over and over again. Now the canoe was midway into the bay. As I looked into the water I saw the shadow of a shark beneath us. It was at least three times the size of the canoe, and it followed us with no effort. As we neared the shallows, it twisted its body around and headed back out into the ocean.

We all jumped out of the canoe, which had beached on the sand, and carried it as fast and far up as we could. We'd worked up a hell of an appetite. Ronnie walked alongside me, a puzzled look on her face.

"You so full of surprises! How long you been paddling canoe?"

It was my turn to be perplexed. "My first time," I said. "I've never paddled a canoe in my life before today."

She smiled enigmatically, nodding her head, as she had that night at Mākaha.

"So," she said, "you saw the shark underneath the canoe?"

I was relieved. I thought I had imagined it.

"You saw it too?" I asked her. "That damn thing was huge!" My mouth was dry.

She still had that distracted half-smile on her face. Finally she said, "That shark was so big that it looked like it was right under us. But it wasn't. It was at least five, maybe ten feet below us."

She stopped abruptly, pointing toward Kūʻīlioloa heiau on the other side of the park.

"Let's go over there and talk. You saw it, so I know I can share this with you." She went to her tent briefly to get a mat and led me away without a word, to me or to her boyfriend.

▼   ▼   ▼

We sat on the second level of the heiau, looking out toward the sea. Ronnie pointed her finger at Nānākuli and swept it around past the two of us.

"From all along that coastline to this heiau is where my 'aumakua swim. It's their domain, and they protect their families." She paused and looked at me intently. "You saw him too, which means you are family also. Somehow we must be related."

So there it was. I looked at her without speaking. I'd known about 'aumakua since I was a kid, but in our family, we were protected by Pele and her older, most sacred brother.

Finally, I asked, "Your 'aumakua. Who is he?"

"Kamohoali'ī," she said.

I gasped. The very same as mine. Pele's older brother. Someone had told me once that there was no such thing as coincidence in life. That was certainly true of Ronnie. She smiled brightly again, reading my mind, and began to unfurl the mat. It was a fine makaloa mat, very rare, and passed down from one generation to the next. She invited me to sit with her, which meant that she now trusted me enough to reveal something very personal and very secret. She told me this story.

"In 1974, I was a senior at Wai'anae, and it was about a month before graduation. My father was so pleased when he knew I'd actually get through high school that he let me drive his Mustang to class one morning. I couldn't believe it. Being a good, dutiful, studious girl, I picked up my cousin, drove right past the high school, and stopped at Mākaha Drive-In. Then we picked up our boyfriends.

"Well, the trip was delayed for another hour. My cousin and I fooled around—ho'oipipo—with our boyfriends. Then we drove off to Keawa'ula Beach—you know, Yokohama.

"The ocean was rough that morning, but I was happy and oblivious, and the first thing I did was run down the sand dune and I dove headfirst into the surf. Swimming seemed easier than usual, and I was past the breaking waves in no time, in the deep. And I just let my body float in the water for what seemed like a minute. I thought of life after graduation. Two years junior college, UH, maybe a part-time job on campus. The world was perfect.

"Slowly, I came out of my trance and started swimming back to shore. Actually, I was treading water, and I looked for my cousin and our two boyfriends, and they were gone. I looked further down the shoreline, and it looked as though they'd moved further off to the right, and it seemed as though they were the size of ants. I looked up to the mountain, and there's a huge globe on top of the ridge, and it looked as though it had moved as well.

"It was a while before I realized that I was the one who had moved. I'd been carried away by a strong current. My father had taught me everything about the ocean, but I couldn't remember anything. I swam frantically, but went nowhere, and kept moving until none of my muscles moved any more. I was so exhausted I couldn't even tread water. I remember thinking that this was a hell of a way to die, that I would drown before graduation.

"My eyes were full of salt and tears, but I suddenly saw a huge fin break through the water, headed straight for me. Just as suddenly, it disappeared into the water. I was sinking, but I saw the shark make three passes alongside me as though sizing up a meal. And then it shot straight down toward the bottom of the ocean. That was the last thing I remembered before I passed out.

"And then I came to on the beach, throwing up sea water and trying to sit up, surrounded by my cousin and the two boys, all in a panic. They told me what had happened, but none of it sank in until days later.

"They'd been sitting on the dune, and they knew I was swimming against the current. All three of them were getting ready to dive in when they saw what my cousin called a shark the size of a baby whale coming right toward me, and they saw me go under. All they could do was stand on the beach, helpless, expecting the worst.

"When the next wave pulled back and peaked, they saw two forms just beneath the wall of the water, which had crashed on the sand with unusual force and a roar like thunder. When the water receded, they saw a very tall, dark Hawaiian man in a red malo, dragging me behind him.

"He dragged me by the hair far up to the beach and left me. He looked at my cousin and smiled. She recalls a wide grin and unusually white teeth. He said nothing, though, and, when he was three steps away from the ocean, another wave appeared as if by magic, covered him completely, and he was gone. About ten feet away from the shore, the shark appeared again, darting quickly toward the horizon.

"We tried to figure out who the man was, since he'd saved me from being killed by a shark. But if I know nothing else, I know this: the man was the shark. And the shark was my 'aumakua."

▼ ▼ ▼

Ronnie generally liked to keep the world at bay, and I was surprised, even now, to see her crying uncontrollably. Eventually, she regained her composure, and she and I basked in the orange glow of the setting sun as we sat on an ancient navigational temple. We both saw a large dark figure, just beneath the ocean's surface, swimming back toward Nānākuli.

Pō Kāne

By the Hawaiian moon calendar, the night of Kāne is the one when the moon is completely absent from the sky. On that night, and that night alone, the nightmarchers walk and, on that night alone, they rule our world.

The first thing you will hear is the sound of drums, distant at first, then louder. You will sense a foul and musky odor in the air—the smell of something that has died—and then see a long line of torchlights that grow larger and brighter. The nightmarchers give you fair warning to get out of their way.

If you stay, you will hear the loud, mournful call of the conch shell—the pū—and you will hear a call—"Kapu moe!"—an order to prostrate yourself. You should remove all of your clothing, and lie face down on the ground and hope. Your best chance is to have an ancestor among them who recognizes you and calls out, "Na'u!" which means "Mine!" If you are in a nightmarcher's bloodline, no one in the procession can harm you.

If you have no ancestors or, even worse, are not Hawaiian, you should urinate into your hand, rub it all over yourself, and then lie naked and face down. This gives you an outside chance of survival.

You see, the nightmarchers are the vanguard for a sacred chief or chiefess, members of the aliʻi, whose unusually high station in life, under the kapu system, required commoners to face down, never casting their eyes upon them. Doing so would invite swift death.

All this seems archaic, even brutal to the modern mind. But history reminds us that even our greatest conqueror and king, Kamehameha, was required to strip naked and crawl to his wife Keopuolani. She was sacred.

Nightmarchers do not only serve the aliʻi. They also serve the gods—the akua and the ʻaumakua. In this capacity, they are more forgiving and less easily offended at breaches of protocol. Their harbingers are enormous gusts of wind, strong enough to tear branches from the largest trees, sudden storms, or fierce downpours whose drops feel like knives.

The trails of the nightmarchers have been traced through private homes, offices, parking lots, and schools, and sometimes even graveyards. When I am asked why, my answer is simple:

"Well," I say, "one thing was done wrong. Someone put these buildings in the middle of their path, and no matter what is built over that path— and even if you bulldoze or somehow change the shape of the land—they will continue to march."

When they do march, they always travel mauka to makai, and never the other way around. They begin in the mountains and head for the ocean. I'm told that they have been seen near volcanoes or water tables. There is a nightmarchers' trail in Moanalua Valley, beginning from the rear of the valley and cutting through Kaiser Hospital, crossing the freeway and continuing through a portion of the Damon Estate. It covers the area behind the 99-Cent Market where, incidentally, the entrance to Pō, the eternal night, begins. It goes through the old Hopaco Building, heading toward milu, the underworld.

Through oversight, or neglect, the entrance to the underworld is at the old Gibson's Store, which closed in the late 80s and where hauntings were reported regularly.

I'm including firsthand accounts from people who have met the nightmarchers and lived to tell the tale, changed remarkably for their pains. If these people were arrogant and full of themselves before, they are not any more, and they all seem to agree that their experience built a certain humility in a way nothing else could.

Kalei Ah Young

For some years, I was a student at my older cousin's hula halau. He often conducted classes in the oddest locations. One night, we went to 'Ewa Beach, to a place known as Haubush.

We had a kumu hula named Keone, who was often away on business and would leave us to practice on our own. We were required, whenever practicing or performing, to wear the traditional malo. This attracted a number of onlookers, most friendly, all harmless.

At Haubush, we had an audience of homeless people who lived on the beach there. After we had finished and changed our clothes and were heading back to our cars, one of them approached us. His name was Kalei Ah Young. He introduced himself and we did the same, without the usual reservations we might have had.

For one thing, he didn't look homeless. Nor did he look ashamed, or angry, or defiant. Watching us, he said, reminded him of something that happened to him in high school.

He had traveled with a wild crowd, he said. They were crazy guys, always drinking and fighting. Because of the liquor laws, they drank in public parks.

One night after a football game, they drove to Haubush and spent the night drinking on the beach. No one noticed that there was no moon to be found in the sky and that it was unusually dark.

By two in the morning, most of the guys had gone home, leaving Kalei and three of his friends on the beach. Kalei wanted more beer, and remembered that there were a few more cases in the car. His two friends ran toward him, waving their hands and screaming, but he didn't understand them and kept walking. They ran full speed toward him and tackled him, pinning him to the ground.

"Stay down! Stay down! No look! No look!" All three were on top of him, holding him down. Then he didn't hear them anymore. Instead, he heard drums—insistent and deafening—and there was a thick, pungent odor, enough to churn the beer in his stomach.

He had to get up or die suffocating, and with his last bit of strength, he twisted away from them. The heat was unbearable, and he tore off his shirt. He inhaled foul air and could only hear the drone of drums and could only see a white mist. Through the haze, Kalei looked back at his friends, who were screaming at him, but he couldn't hear them. Then something grabbed hold of him, forcing him down with such enormous strength that he was completely winded.

His breathing became shallow, and he felt a piercing, burning sensation above his right hip. His body was forcibly twisted to the left, causing him so much pain that he couldn't scream. It all lasted less than a minute, but it felt like eternity, and before he could make any sense of it at all, it was all over. The mist was gone, the air was fresh and clear, and the drumming had stopped. All he had left now was the throbbing pain as his friends looked at him in sorrow and regret, as though he had been shot.

Even proud men cry, and Kalei did as he told the story. It was, he said, the time of the nightmarchers. Their path extends through Haubush all the way to Kalaeloa. His friends, he said, had seen a long line of torches, and tried to stop him.

"I'll show you something," he told us. "Get flashlight?"

Somebody got one from a car. "Point right here," said Kalei, turning and showing his bare back.

Just above his hip was a footprint, larger than life, so complete that the ball of the foot, its arch, and all five toes, right down to the prints, were as clear as day. It had been burned onto his skin.

"They left this to remind me of my mistake," he said quietly. We would not learn much more about Kalei, as he turned then and left us, but we were very quiet on the way home. Papers and social scientists have a lot of statistics about the homeless. All we would remember for years to come was what he told us in parting, and we would never practice on the night of Kāne.

Caught in the Path

There's something about summer that attracts the ghostly and the supernatural. Maybe it's the atmosphere, or the fact that the moon is closer to the earth. Then again, maybe I'm looking for a clear and logical explanation for something that happened to me back in July of 2001.

A few friends and I had gathered at the Chinese cemetery in Pauoa. We'd heard stories of hauntings there—babies crying, green orbs of light streaking through the graveyard, and one involving a young Chinese girl dressed in red, floating over the headstones.

At first, we found nothing, even with our meters. We even checked our digital cameras. We had portable voice recorders, but they only played back traffic and some rather loud and animated conversations from the apartment down the street.

Then we went down to Pauoa stream, near a large banyan tree. We were very close to the caretakers' residence, a family named Aikau.

Some of us believed that banyan trees attract lost spirits, giving them a permanent home. Those who did used all the equipment they could, photographing and recording to their hearts' content. These people meant well, but they were amateurs, kids in a candy store, soldiers charging into battle with blinders on.

Somehow I felt like their father, as they haphazardly clicked, wrote, read temperature changes, and scurried about like children at Christmas in search of one more present. I just wanted to be sure that none of them got hurt.

Suddenly, the weather changed, and it was hotter than hell. And as I gazed at the banyan tree through the uncomfortable heat, I noticed the wind ripping through the cemetery, strong enough to bend the tree over to one side. Then I realized that I couldn't hear anything. And I couldn't feel the wind.

The group began to scatter away from the tree, against the powerful wind, fighting it, and sweating and gesturing and shouting at me.

I then realized that it had become boiling hot. I still couldn't hear or feel the wind, but I could tell by the looks on their faces that they were frightened for me, and I suddenly felt all alone in a vortex, stunned and powerless. It felt like infinity.

To this day, I can't tell you what it was that kept me there, except that whatever it was was invisible. But as suddenly as it grabbed me, it released me and disappeared, and I crumpled into the grass exhausted. The group surrounded me, and some were crying. "Don't be ridiculous," I said, in a voice that was shaking and ridiculously loud. "I'm not dead."

I struggled gamely to my feet. The heat was gone, and a cool breeze flowed through the graveyard in its place. And all at once, I could hear again. I heard my friends chattering, all at once. One of them asked me what had happened.

"I don't know," I said, still dazed. "You tell me."

An hour later we were at Zippy's. I had inhaled two Pepsis and two bowls of saimin, and I was beginning to breathe normally again. I was back in control. I figured that the most reliable member of the group was a guy named Todd, who had seen it first. He told me that I was maybe ten feet away from the tree, and they saw me seem to disappear in pillars of white mist, while another column of mist passed me by. They tried to get to me, but the fierce winds kept them back. When the mist disappeared, they figured I was probably okay.

I thanked them all for trying to rescue me; they were a great bunch of guys. Then I asked, almost offhandedly, "Did anyone take a picture?" Their silence answered the question for me.

A year or so later, I went to a lecture on nightmarchers at the Office of Native Affairs. I sat as inconspicuously as possible in back of the room.

Most of the lecture was old hat for even a novice ghosthunter. But I did learn that what happened to me in Pauoa had also happened to others before me.

The rest is all an educated guess. I'd been caught in the middle of the nightmarchers' path. I felt hot and had been unable to hear the wind because I must have been recognized by some of my ancestors among them, who had called out my name, surrounded me, and protected me until the procession passed. And the wind that had kept my friends back were their ancestors—they were all Hawaiian—holding them back, protecting them as well.

It would be impossible to say whether it was a procession of the gods or the ali'i. It really doesn't matter. What does is that my friends and I are alive to tell the tale, and the fact that we have no pictures doesn't matter one bit.

Waiting for a Hot Date

I heard this story from a woman named Kapunohu, who lives in Kona with her kid brother Poni. "Kolohe kid," she laughed. "But good."

One night she came home after work; the sun was down and it was pitch black out. She pulled her car into the front yard and saw her brother Poni standing in front of the porch. He was dressed in a pair of clean white jeans, his favorite red and white aloha shirt, and his only pair of good shoes. He'd slicked his hair back. Something was up.

"Wow, where you going?" she laughed.

"Hot date," Poni said. "I waiting fo' my new haole girlfriend."

"Haole girlfriend? I hope she understand what you saying!" She ribbed him whenever she could.

"Ah, shaddup. I can turn on da English when I like!" She barely heard him; she was already in the house and headed for the shower. It had been an unusually long workday and, thankfully, the last one of the week. She was meeting some friends at

Sam Choy's and planning a late movie. She was dressed and ready by a quarter to seven.

Because it was so dark out, the porch light was good only to the bottom of the stairs. Kapunoho crossed the front yard, tripped, and fell. Cursing, she looked back and saw the figure of a man curled up in fetal position, crying hysterically. When she recognized her brother, she screamed, but regained her composure, holding him, trying to get him up, trying to remember the number of the hospital.

Poni seemed all right after a few minutes, but Kapunohu saw something around his neck. She looked long and hard at it, and realized that it was their great-grandmother's lei niho palaoa—a whale tooth pendant with a necklace of braided human hair.

She gasped. "Aha-hana!" They looked at each other, and finally she said, almost forgivingly, "Sometimes, Poni, you more trouble than you worth." The pendant was not only precious, but sacred. For generations it had survived in their family. In ancient times, a chief had worn it proudly, to signify his status.

"Gonfannit dopey brother of mine," she said. "So tell me how come you did this?"

Poni's eyes were dry now, but they had no defiance in them, and he was limp and slow.

"This haole girl. I mean it, she's really pretty— a knockout. Very special, you know?"

His sister nodded. "So I kinda wanted to impress her. Hawaiian, you know? So I thought of this," he continued, holding the pendant. "I mean, I thought it would be cool."

"So I put it on, and funny thing. It looked real good, but I started to tingle, and I thought I was just nervous. So I come out, and get this real funny kine smell, like ten thousand mongoose wen die right here. And then, well you not gonna believe..."

Kapunohu patted him gently on the back. "I believe. Go on."

"Okay. What I saw—I was looking off to the left—I saw torches, and it looked like they were all the way down to Kealakekua. I forgot I had a date. I coulda sworn I heard drums all over the place, but I'm not sure. So I walked down the driveway to see what was happening. Torches, drumming. Maybe a parade. I come back into the yard and I see this guy. One old Hawaiian warrior. Must have been seven feet tall. This guy'd been watching me, and he was pissed. I thought first it was a joke, but I knew it wasn't. The guy's feet—get this—they disappeared below his knees, like there was nothing there. Spooky, yeah?"

Kapunohu nodded, and Poni went on. "I couldn't even yell or scream. The guy's eyes were burning. The guy's arms were bigger than me. And then he said to me, ' 'O wai la 'oe? 'O wai la 'oe? 'O wai la 'oe?' I know he's asking me, 'Who are you?' over and over and over again, and he was pointing at my chest.

"I can't say anything, but when he takes his canoe paddle and swings it at my head, man I duck. Right here on the ground. Must have been about that time you tripped over me."

Kapunohu explained to me what she had told her brother. The warrior ghost knew the pendant, but because Pohi had been too frightened to answer, he did the only thing he could. Lucky for him she tripped on him. For some reason, the warrior knew who she was, and disappeared.

▼ ▼ ▼

Poni went upstairs to shower, and his new girlfriend came up the driveway. Kapunohu welcomed her in the house and kept her company, not mentioning, of course, what had just happened.

Poni changed into the only other decent clothes he had. They were his church clothes. Dark slacks, a button-down blue Oxford shirt, and, since his favorite shoes had been scuffed, a pair of polished coroframs—military boots he'd gotten from a surplus shop—which he tried to cover with his slacks. He went down the stairs slowly, feeling awkward and uncomfortable.

But when he saw her, he exchanged glances with his sister, whose face beamed approval. This would be a great relationship. She wore a red and white aloha shirt and a pair of white jeans. "Fo' one haole," Kapunohu told me, "she was perfect."

Skin-Deep

Phillip DeCoito grew up in Wainaku, a plantation town just outside Hilo. He told me this story a couple of years ago, simple and direct. But every now and then he'd pause, as though frightened he might bring the story's characters back from the dead. Anyway, this is how it goes.

It happened when Phillip was seven. His father worked at the sugar mill and his mother took care of the house. In those days, when extra hands were needed in the fields, wives would work alongside their husbands.

One afternoon, Phillip did his usual homework and chores before bathing, and then joined the family for supper. For him, the best part of the meal was his mother's bread, which was a legend in Wainaku. Paodoce bread—sweet, always fresh. Better than any bakery.

It was a special favorite of the plantation boss's wife, who would come by for a loaf or two, and although she insisted on paying, Mrs. DeCoito refused. One day, though, when she dropped by for bread, she told Mrs. DeCoito that she had to take the money. The bread, she said, reminded her of her mother's bread when she was a child in Pukalani. It was that good, she said, forcing the money into her hand.

Now Mrs. DeCoito was naturally nosy, and often thought of asking the woman about her family on Maui. But there was, in those days, an unseen wall of reserve between managers' families and those of the workers, even in each others' houses. Besides, she thought, it would be rude.

All plantation towns were run largely by rumor, and Wainaku was no exception. There were many about the manager's wife, especially because she was uncommonly beautiful—no one else on the island came close—and had fair skin, never darkened by the sun. She had green eyes like a cat and perfectly-shaped brows arched over them, a mane of red hair, and naturally red lips. Most of the men in Wainaku would have traded half their lifespans to spend a moment with her.

This rumor was true, Phillip told me: when she was nineteen, still living in Pukalani, her father sent her to live in Hilo with his brother and his family. He had been concerned about the number of young men, many of them with expensive gifts and hopeful eyes who came to their door, and the fact that most of them were engaged or married. His daughter had rapidly, innocently, and unwittingly earned the spite and enmity of all the women in Pukalani. After a few years in Hilo, thought her father, she would mature, and might return home safely.

She was responsible in Hilo. She cooked, cleaned, helped care for her two younger cousins, both boys, and was altogether pleasant. But her aunt became testy and unsettled. For one thing, she was too beautiful—much more so than the letters and photographs from her father on Maui could have shown—and she was in Hilo for vague, unspecified reasons. And her aunt often caught her husband and her niece exchanging quick, furtive glances.

It all came to a head one Tuesday afternoon. All the housework had been finished, and her aunt was preparing dinner, so the young woman played chase master in the yard with her cousins. The kids played rough, and one of the boys pulled her hair hard. In a sudden flash of anger, the first they had ever seen from her, she slapped them both hard on the face, raising welts. Her aunt, hearing their screams, hurried into the yard.

"She slapped us, Mommy!" the two boys said in tandem. Without a word, the girl's aunt slapped her, swearing in Portuguese. "You are a whore!" she shrieked. "You are a servant of the devil!"

Her uncle had just gotten home, and got an animated earful from his wife. He paid her no mind. He went to the girl, held her in his arms, and reassured her. Her aunt watched this with disgust, then shock, and decided that the girl had to leave for Maui the next day.

That night the girl was packing her clothes, and she heard a knock on the door. It was the manager himself, coming to ask for more hands for an irrigation ditch. He looked long and hard at the girl. "Will you come, too? We need all the hands we can get."

She agreed. A week later she was the manager's wife.

Phillip's mother didn't care one way or the other. "All rumors," she would say. "She neva' do nothing to me. She always buy bread from my kitchen and she nice to me. Das all I know." And once, she added, "But if you like talk about somebody, how bout da plantation manager? Hah? Now das one story!"

▼ ▼ ▼

The manager was thirty-four when he met and married the girl from Pukalani. Until then he had been a confirmed bachelor. Naturally, every matchmaker from Wainaku to Keaʻau tried to find him a wife. He went out occasionally to a dance or a party, but nothing serious ever happened.

In fact, even an old fatseda—the rough Portuguese equivalent of a kahuna or a witch—tried to arrange a match between the manager and her daughter. The daughter, a bit plain, was eager, but the manager was not, and the manager finally told her mother bluntly that he was afraid her daughter's looks might be inherited by their children if they married.

About three nights later, he had a nightmare—one in which the old fatseda slipped through his bedroom door yelling Portuguese curses: "Meldish! Meldish!" She grabbed the sides of his face and dug her long nails into his cheeks. The manager tried to yell for help, but no sound would come from his mouth, and he was unable to move.

When he woke the following morning, he went into the bathroom and saw his face reflected in the mirror. There were scratches on it, three on each side.

In short, where love was concerned, the manager had concluded that it was more trouble than it was worth, until he met the girl from Pukalani.

"How dat for one story?" Mrs. DeCoito would ask.

Phillip would always remember something about the manager's wife. After they were married, she wore jewelry, shiny earrings, and a gold chain with a red stone—the sort of jewelry one wouldn't even see in Honolulu.

One evening, Mrs. DeCoito was half-expecting the manager's wife to come by for bread. No one showed, that evening or the next. Late on the second night, Phillip saw his parents at the kitchen table, and his mother was sobbing.

"Ma, what's wrong?" he asked. His father waved him off gently.

"You know da lady who buy paodoce from Mommy? She wen make. Dead, last night."

"Make? But how come, Daddy?"

"We dunno, boy, we dunno." His father sighed. "Your mommy was her only friend, I guess. Nobody wen like her, nobody talk to her. Even though she da manager's wife. Mommy the only one she talk to." Looking at his wife sadly, he said, "And so young too, yeah, honey? Only thirty-five. Ho, puating, I tell you."

In those days, people had wakes. This one was sadder than most. No one came except for the manager—about fifty by now, looking much older— a priest from another parish down the road, Phillip, and his mother. The manager's wife was dressed in black with a dark shawl covering her hands. She had every piece of jewelry she had ever owned—rings, bracelets, broaches, pendants, earrings—in the coffin with her, almost a grotesque caricature. Phillip knew he was supposed to be sad, but all he could think was this: where was the thanks?

Where was the thanks? Jeez, his mother was her only friend, and nothing at all for her. He grew angry, and when he got home the anger had turned into cold fury. He went to bed and pretended to be asleep until the house was quiet. He then took his pillow out of the case, put on jeans and a t-shirt, and slowly climbed out of his bedroom window. It was the night of no moon, something the Hawaiians call Kāne.

He ran swiftly through the neighborhood, taking care to avoid houses with dogs or chickens in the yard, until he was at the rear of the manager's house. He heard the manager snoring fitfully, and he poked a small hole into the screen with a penknife. In slow motion, he removed the hook and made a crack in the window just large enough to squeeze through.

He made it in with some effort. He had never realized how big the manager's house was. He tiptoed into the living room. All he'd meant to do was filch a ring or a bracelet. But his anger rose again. He systematically removed everything—down to the last pearl—and put it in the pillowcase. He slid back to the window, put his leg out, and noticed with alarm that the snoring had stopped.

He slid slowly through the window, making no sound. He was shaking now. He thought he saw a shadow pass by in another window and began to hear arguing—loud voices, a woman's voice among them. He couldn't make out the words. Then he heard the manager yell, "Go away! Go away! Leave me alone!" My God, Phillip thought, is he having an argument with himself? He'd heard stories like that from his friends, but never believed them. He was free of the window now, and ran like the wind. For some reason, he stopped for a second to look back, and he saw a figure at the back window. It was too large to be the manager. The figure locked the screen and closed the window.

He climbed through his window, and the house was still quiet. He slid the pillowcase under his mattress and thought about how he would surprise his mother next birthday.

Three days went by, and Phillip had nearly forgotten that night. At dinner, there was a knock at the back door. Mrs. DeCoito opened it; no one was there. "Must have been the wind," she said. There was another knock, and she sighed and opened it again. She would say later she felt strange, as though the manager's wife was coming for bread.

Again there was nothing, but the knocking continued, all around the house, growing unbearably loud, almost deafening. The three DeCoitos stood in shock, wondering if there was an earthquake from the volcano and if they would have to evacuate.

The knocking stopped, then it appeared again as it had, quietly, at the back door. Phillip's father opened the door this time. He saw a woman, dressed in black, head down, covered by a shawl. His father didn't scare easily. "You need sometin'?"

"Phillip," said the woman, in a voice that sounded drunken and subdued. "The boy, Phillip."

"Whatchoo like wit him?"

"He has some things that belong to me. I want them back." Phillip's father shook a bit. This was not the sort of practical joke seen in plantation towns. Phillip had never seen his father shake before.

His father turned to him, trying to keep one eye on the woman at the door. "Boy, this lady outside. You heard?" Phillip nodded, and as he did, the woman raised her veil. He saw her face, and screamed—the sort of scream no parent should ever hear from their child. Mrs. DeCoito grabbed him and pulled him away.

"Mrs. DeCoito?" said the woman in a singsong voice. "Your boy has my things. Give them back to me."

His mother stood, arms on her hips, her voice quavering only slightly. "Holy Mary, mother of God, all the saints, Lord protect us! Eh, I got no bread for you. Understand? No bread! Get out of here and leave us alone!" And with that, the woman dissolved and vanished.

Phillip explained everything to his parents, and told them why, but this did not save him from the sting of his father's belt. He would remember it as the worst punishment he'd ever had.

His parents arranged for the return of the jewelry through the priest, whom they knew. But the manager's wife had been buried the day before. They were religious, and decided to visit the manager himself and confess. The manager was a decent man, and wouldn't hold their son's waywardness against them. They took Phillip with them, marching, as if at gunpoint.

The manager listened to them, with a sad smile on his face. Finally he said, "You know, you're lucky she didn't grab you by the throat and choke you! God, she was a selfish one." He turned, almost paternally, to Phillip. "I can see that you love your mother very much." His mother kicked him gently and Phillip looked at him.

"Yes, sir."

"Well, son," said the manager, "my wife did too, you know. Your mother was her only friend in this world."

Phillip no longer felt uneasy. "How come?" he asked.

This time his father nudged him. "No be niele, son."

The manager waved his hand as though to dismiss the matter. "It's okay." He paused for a bit, and it seemed to Phillip as though a priest was confessing to him, an odd sensation at his age.

"It's okay," the manager repeated. "Her parents died soon after she left Pukalani. There was nothing for her to go home to. "Lucky, I guess, that we needed extra hands for the irrigation ditch then. When I saw her, I knew...well, you know." Phillips parents nodded slowly in unison.

"Anyway, her uncle was the only real family she had left, and he—how should I put this—did not treat his niece the way an uncle should treat his niece." There was a long silence. "On top of that, I found out he beat his wife and children. I had him kicked out of the area, and his wife left him. I think she's in Kona."

"Can I ask—can I ask how she died?" asked Phillip

After a long pause, the manager said, "I think she simply got tired of living. I mean, her parents gone, just like that. And the rumors. A year or so of those and she stayed inside almost all the time, and there was nothing I could do to reach her. The only true happiness she enjoyed was the jewelry her parents had left her and your mother's bread."

The manager was looking at the floor now, and Phillip thought he might be crying. He had never seen a man cry before, and he shifted uncomfortably.

Mrs. DeCoito said, in an uncharacteristically gentle voice, "But she was so beautiful."

"Yes," said the manager. "But she never felt that way. Her past, and the whispering, and the stories—beauty can't get anybody through that."

Suddenly he stood up, a man in command again. "Mr. DeCoito, come see me at the end of the week. I've got a new position for you, I think." He smiled at them. "You're good people, all of you."

The DeCoitos left, relieved and in good spirits, and they all went to bed immediately. In the middle of the night, Phillip felt a weight pushing him into his bed, nearly choking him, and he meant to say, "But I gave you back your jewelry" but thought it instead.

The woman's voice, almost narcotic in tone, said, "I know you did, and thank you. Because if you hadn't, you'd be in the coffin with me right now."

Then Phillip was free, and for a minute was silent. Then he screamed again, the sort of scream that no parent should ever hear from their child.

▼   ▼   ▼

That was the story he told me. And he was a man now, middle-aged and weathered, and he was late for something. He hopped into his old Camaro and drove toward Hilo. I followed him and noticed he was turning into the graveyard outside town. He had some flowers as he stepped out of the car, and I parked a ways behind him. Phillip could be touchy sometimes. But I could see the headstones, which read:

Walter DeCoito and his beloved Wife Mary Roseline Fernandez DeCoito, both born in the Year Of Our Lord 1901, Married 50 years. Walter departed this earth in 1982. Mary departed this earth in 1997. They rest in the kingdom of heaven.

There was a wind playing softly around me, a late afternoon Hilo wind. I knew I had to get back to my room at the Naniloa to pack; I was returning to Honolulu the next morning. I looked around and saw no sign of Phillip. But I did smell something like freshly baked bread, so strongly that I wanted to reach out into the air and pull out a piece. But there was none to pull.

I packed and spent a somber evening at a restaurant full of customers and clattering dishes. I felt even lonelier the next morning on the plane, and hoped the feeling wouldn't last. There was work to be done.

That evening, back in Honolulu, I went to Kaimana Beach. It was almost empty except for a few couples and a body surfer.

There is an ancient Hawaiian cleansing ceremony called Pīkai. One allows the outgoing water from the ocean to clear away all the bad things—sickness, troubled heart, old demons. I floated upon the water and thought briefly of how many over thousands of years had done the same, and had seen the same stars I was seeing now. I thanked my ancestors for the work. And I thanked those who have passed into the next world for letting me tell their stories plain, simple, and direct with no embellishments. It was good to be home.

Lunalilo

King William Charles Lunalilo's reign was brief—less than a year. He died young, a bachelor, and was the last member of his house to rule Hawai'i. His remains are kept in a mausoleum at Kawaiaha'o Church, and his tomb is magnificent.

He died in 1874. Every year, on the anniversary of his passing, the tomb is opened for kind of a spring cleaning. The only people allowed in are the kahu—the keepers—and select members of the church, along with members of the Chiefly Orders and Royal Societies.

I'm told that the interior of the king's tomb is beautiful and ornate. It is made entirely of wood, although I'm not sure what kind. On each side, save for the front, there are captivating stained glass windows.

I've also heard that the king's crown jewels were kept inside the tomb. But no one really knows, except for the few who are allowed inside each year, and these people will take the secret to their own graves.

Two thieves came close. Honolulu is a small town, and somehow they found out about the jewels. If they could get them somehow, they could be fenced outside Hawai'i, perhaps in Europe or South America.

They parked their car one night on Mililani Street, a dark, dimly lit street, and reviewed their plans in low whispers. They were apprehensive but optimistic, with dreams of sudden and limitless wealth spurring them on.

They climbed over the back wall of the mausoleum and found themselves at the tomb's rear window. One of them broke the stained glass window with a hammer, and one of them helped the other climb into the tomb, looking all the while for witnesses or police, seeing none. In fact, there would be no witnesses at all.

Early the next morning, the caretaker would find their bodies in back of the mausoleum. One of them had been badly beaten, and the other had not, but both their necks were broken. The caretaker would never forget that morning, try as he might.

The cops could only speculate. Their first theory was that the thief standing watch on the outside must have heard something, looked in, seen his battered friend, and jumped in through the window to help. It was all pretty hazy. The only thing they could agree on was that whoever was inside the tomb was huge, larger than their own skeptical minds could imagine. "Herculean," remarked one of the medical examiners. The report was inconclusive. It mentioned the unusually large fingerprints on the thief's left wrist, indicating that he was not resisting, but trying to escape. His ribs had been crushed so badly that on autopsy, shards of bone were found in his lungs and liver. And, of course, both their necks were broken.

King Lunalilo's reign was tragically short, but his legacy meant to last forever. The mausoleum stands today as it did a hundred and thirty years ago, a testament to a king who so loved his people that his final wish was to be buried among them. The wooden doors of the tomb are protected by iron gates, which are locked like hands in prayer, silent, secret, devout.

Family

There is only one Pele. For many Hawaiians, she is the mother of us all, and those who know her warn you to be very careful around her. She is, after all, the volcanic goddess. She deserves and gets proper respect.

▼ ▼ ▼

Back in January of '92, some friends and I needed material and information for a play based on Kalapana, so we went to the Big Island. Some of us went for spiritual reasons; others for the sheer pleasure of the trip. Some had genuine encounters with the supernatural and others did not. There were others who feigned experience when in fact nothing at all had happened to them. Human beings have a strong need to belong.

My moment of truth came when someone took my picture. I was standing at Halemaʻumaʻu, and the sacred cliff of Pele's brother, Kamohoaliʻi, king of sharks. It was he who guided Pele on her canoe from Kahiki to Hawaiʻi.

When I saw the picture, I saw, right behind me, a swirl of smoke. And in that smoke you can see the face of a fierce Hawaiian man right next to me. I am not certain, of course, that it was Kamohoali'ī.

But I do know that my late Auntie Ella told me that she was a haka, a medium, for Kamohoali'ī. Sometimes, he would enter her body in order to speak to other people through her. She said that he had a sense of humor, and tried to put people at ease, so they would not be afraid of him. Shortly before she died, Auntie remembered that our 'aumakua had a favorite song—a modern Hawaiian one. He would often ask someone to sing it for him. I never found out the name of the song.

But if a modern Hawaiian song is favored by an 'aumakua, this proves that the 'aumakua is real, still among us, listening and watching.

And if I needed further proof, I would find it in 1998. My wife had won a weekend stay at a Kona resort for her, our daughter, and me.

Whenever I visit the Big Island, I make it a point to pay my respects to Pele at the volcano and then to Kamohoali'ī at Kawaihae. I wanted my daughter to see these places as well, to find out where she and her people are from. We visited Pu'ukoholā at Kawaihae, and I carried my daughter down to the bay, which is below a great temple. I told her that our family temple was somewhere in the ocean, very close by, only a few feet away. Immediately, the heads of seven turtles popped up from under the water, looking directly at her.

For the rest of the afternoon, she played and frolicked at Spencer Beach Park, perfectly at home. No one seemed to notice the white pueo—an owl— perched in the high branches of a nearby kiawe tree. No one, except me. We made eye contact, the two of us, and the bird seemed to nod in my direction, acknowledging me. I nodded back to him and thanked him for his presence.

And then it was time to go. I looked back at the pueo for one last goodbye, but he was gone.

Someone once said that we tell stories in order to live. My daughter has heard a lot of stories of our people, who were at one with themselves and their environment. Her name is Hiwalani, and it means "Descendant of Royal Esteem." Her name, I hope, will ensure that everyone she meets in life will treat her well. More importantly, though, I cherish the hope that her ancestors—especially the goddess Pele— will watch over her and guide her toward the correct path in life. And so far, they have.

Sources

Fornander, Abraham. 2004. *Fornander Collection of Hawaiian Antiquities and Folklore.* Bishop Museum Press, Honolulu.

Sterling, Eslpeth C. and Catherine C. Summers. 1978. *Sites of Oʻahu.* Bishop Museum Press, Honolulu.

———. 1964. In Samuel Kamakau, *Ka Poʻe Kahiko: The People of Old.* Bishop Museum Special Publication 51. Honolulu.

Malo, David. 1987. 2nd edition. *Hawaiian Antiquities.* Bishop Museum Press, Honolulu.

About the Author

Robert Lopaka Kapanui is a teacher's assistant at Kawaiahaʻo School and a teller of ghost stories. A hula dancer, member of the Koʻolau Lodge of F&AM, and of the Royal Order of Kamehameha, Kapanui has been featured in two independent films—*The Red Hibiscus,* and *2*—for Pacific Islanders in Communication and Pennybacker Creative, LLC. He is currently directing another PIC short film titled *A Pagan Tattooed Savage.*

His most precious moments are spent with his wife and daughter.